SEEDS OF WAR

BOOK 3

BITTER HARVEST

A Semper Fi Press Book

A Semper Fi Press Book

ISBN-13: 978-1-945743-28-3
ISBN-10: 1-945743-28-X

Printed in the United States of America

This is a work of fiction. All of the characters, names,
incidents, organizations, and dialogue in this work are
either the products of the authors' imagination or are
used fictitiously.

Edited by by James Caplan, Micky Cocker, and
Kelly O'Donnell.

Cover by Jesh Snow

Seeds of War — Book III: Bitter Harvest

Part I: Weeds Amidst the Rubble

Duke whined as Colby stood at the apron, watching the shuttle come in for a landing. The dog had been glued to him since the end of the battle.

"It's OK, girl," he said. "They're the good guys."

Lieutenant Colonel Manuel Sifuentes, Colby's former protégé and the senior active duty Marine left on New Mars, had been trying to organize what remained of the planet's only major city in the aftermath of the battle with the plant soldiers, and the last thing he needed was to worry about the contact team from Earth. Without a real job, Colby had volunteered to meet them. As a retired lieutenant general, he'd had plenty of practice dealing with bureaucrats while still on active duty, and if this could free up Sifuentes, then Colby was happy to help.

No, not "happy." "Willing" would be a better description.

He patted his front pocket where he'd put the list. Government bureaucrats could be—and usually were—a pain in the ass, but they could also get things done. He and Sifuentes had come up with a prioritized list to fix the mess that New Mars had become. The list was not all-inclusive, just what they needed to address the immediate concerns. He had no idea who was on the shuttle, but he was going to give whoever it was the list and get them going on it. Like most bureaucrats, they'd have their own ideas and priorities, no doubt conceived without a proper understanding of the situation here on the ground; Colby's task was to delay or possibly derail their objectives and get the things on his list done right away, even if he had to beg or browbeat them into it.

The shuttle slowly landed, kicking up dust that still had a tinge of green. During the heat of the battle with the plant army, a green mist, created from the bodies of dead plants, had risen, coating everything. Now, a day later, most of it had disappeared. If it were not for the utter destruction of the city, he could have thought that all of the fighting had been a dream. Almost all traces of the plant soldiers themselves were gone.

The shuttle door opened, and the steps unfolded. First to debark were two Capital Guards who rushed down, then took up positions at the bottom of the steps, facing inboard.

Colby kept his face neutral. Like all Marines, he had a very low opinion of the SUTAs (Sticks-Up-The-Ass). They were wannabees, peacocks in fancy uniforms who strutted and pranced, chests puffed out as they reveled in their self-importance. Marines tended to ignore them, but their presence always meant that someone high on the food chain was around.

Someone aboard the shuttle was powerful enough to rate their own praetorian guard, and that changed the equation a bit. He wasn't going to be able to browbeat them into getting his list filled. Colby had lots of experience dealing with the type, and usually the best course of action was to convince the bigwig that whatever Colby wanted had been what they wanted in the first place.

He plastered a smile on his face and thought about skimming the list of likely high-ranking politicians who might be arriving, but his implant had been offline since the battle with the plant daikaiju. His patience, like his smile, was manufactured, but sufficient as he waited to see who had decided to make a personal appearance on the scene. Whoever it was, Colby would just have to deal with them.

An underling, bright and eager, popped her head out of the shuttles hatch, spotted Colby, and ducked back inside. His smile faded just a bit, and he had to force it back to full wattage.

Many of the high and mighty were sticklers for protocol. The fact that there were two capital guards standing at attention at the bottom of the steps meant that whoever was in the shuttle was high-ranking, and that they expected to be met by the appropriate party, not a scruffy-looking farmer and his dog. If he was still on active duty and in full uniform, with an honor guard behind him, that would have satisfied any visiting dignitary, but not as he was now.

He expected an underling to come out first to see who he was and if he was befitting of receiving the head of this group. This nonsense was just wasting time while his list burned a hole in his pocket. He was tempted to march up to the shuttle and announce himself. Even retired, a lieutenant general still carried some weight, and maybe throwing his around wouldn't be such a bad thing.

He'd just taken a step forward when two more guards appeared, stopping at the top of the steps, then turned inboard.

Colby raised his eyebrows in surprise. Maybe this was going to work out after all. Blinded by his own prejudices, he might have judged too soon. Not everyone who was serving at the top levels was an asshole, and if they were willing to come out to meet someone who looked as common as he did now. . .

Colby's optimistic spin reverted to his original judgement of "asshole" as a familiar face appeared at the shuttle's hatch.

Vice-Minister Asahi Greenstein took a moment to look over the wrecked landscape, before settling his gaze on Colby, a half-smile on his face.

This was the corrupt piece of crap who'd ruined Colby's career. All the rage and hatred that Colby thought he'd worked through during his time spent farming on Vasquez surged in him, as fresh as if everything had happened just yesterday.

He would have expected literally anyone else, from the lowest government flack to the commander in chief, anyone besides the vice-minister. The man rarely left the confines of the capital complex on Earth. He was not a "field guy."

But, in a way, this made sense. Colby had sent a report to the vice-minister from Vasquez, so Greenstein would have been among the first to know that humanity had been invaded by an alien species. He'd have had a jump on his rivals, and in the never-ending game of state, that could have huge benefits down the road. That big an opportunity for self-advancement could have been enough to get Greenstein out from behind his desk and into a war zone.

Colby hated the man, but he could still use him. The vice-minister certainly had the heft to get everything on his list filled and then some.

His face ached with the smile he'd plastered on as he watched the man walk down the steps, trailed by the top two guards. As soon as he stepped foot on the ground, the bottom two SUTAs performed an immaculate facing movement in unison, stepping off to precede Greenstein as the five walked up to him.

"Vice-Minister Greenstein, it is good to see you here," Colby said, hand outstretched.

The vice-minister looked at Colby's hand as if it were a rotten piece of meat, then said, "Mister Edson, I am surprised to see you here. Most criminals flee the site of their crimes."

"Excuse me?" Colby asked as his smile slid from his face, replaced by an expression of confusion, his hand still outstretched.

"I might be surprised, but I am grateful. It saves me the trouble of searching for you." He turned to one of the four expressionless SUTAs and said, "Guard Captain Heuhn, arrest this man."

****

Colby ran his tongue over his lip. It was puffy, and he could taste the coppery tang of his blood. The guards had been both brutal and efficient, overwhelming him before he'd had a chance to adequately defend himself. Four-against-one odds had certainly worked against him as well.

He'd gotten in a few shots, and he was pretty sure Duke had bitten one of them, but he'd borne the brunt of the fight, and now, hands cuffed behind him, his body was protesting. At least Duke had gotten away. He hoped she was OK, but if he found out they'd hurt her, there would be hell to pay.

Not that you can do much about it, Edson, locked in this room. They hold all the cards.

He still didn't know why he'd been arrested. Greenstein had beamed while his guards took Colby down, a look of eager anticipation in his eyes. The vice-minister had enjoyed it, like some well rehearsed fantasy, Colby realized.

Two of the guards handcuffed and laid Colby on the deck while the other pair went to find a "jail cell," as the vice-minister told them. Three civilians came out of the shuttle and stood glancing down at Colby, staring at him as if he was a rabid dog. He didn't give them the pleasure of reacting in the least.

Unless there were more civilians in the shuttle, this was a very small contact team to start the recovery ops. Something wasn't adding up, and not just the fact that he'd been arrested. He just couldn't figure out what was going on.

After a long half-hour, the two guards came back with a report of a suitable room. Greenstein waved them off and returned to the shuttle, followed by his three minions.

"You gonna walk?" the guard captain had asked, at least giving him the choice.

What had the vice-minister called him? Heuhn? Maybe he wasn't a total peacock after all.

They led him several blocks through the ruined city to the remains of a small, one-story building. The front was smashed, but the back was still intact. They took him to a good-sized room and sat him down in a chair, hands behind his back.

The four left him in the room, but Colby wasn't naive enough to think he was really alone. He tested his cuffs, more because it was expected of him than in hopes he could break free, then settled in to wait.

He drifted off to sleep, so he wasn't sure how much time had elapsed when a guard opened the door and the vice-minister entered.

The guard exited the room and closed the door behind Greenstein, leaving Colby alone with him. The vice-minister pulled up a chair in front of Colby, turned it around, then sat on it, legs straddling the back and arms crossed over the top.

"You really screwed up, Mister Edson."

Colby didn't say a word. The vice-minister was trying to get a rise out of him, calling him "mister" instead of "general." Normally, Colby would have reacted and corrected him, but there was nothing to be gained by it given the situation. Colby recognized it for what it was: nothing but pettiness on the vice-minister's part.

"Did you really think you could conspire against humanity?" the vice-minister asked. "And you being an ex-Marine at that. I'm shocked."

Greenstein was playing a game, and Colby remained silent, waiting to see where the man was going.

"I've been trying to figure out what you hoped to gain by starting a war with an alien species. At first, I thought it might simply be anger at how your life has turned out. But then, traitor though you are, you've always had ulterior motives. So, I wondered. Maybe an investigation into your financial holdings would reveal something?"

Really? I don't have enough to my name to cover the cost of next year's seeds.

"We finally make first contact, and you instigate a war. Panic ensues, and certain stocks skyrocket. Am I warm?"

Colby said nothing.

"Oh, I've got my investigators working on it. They are very good, Mr. Edson, and they will find what whatever I tell them to."

Shit. Yeah, I'm sure they will.

"You know, there's a record of my report to you from Vasquez," Colby said, unable to keep quiet any longer.

"Oh, you mean this one?" The vice-minister pulled out his compad and looked at it. "It says here that you are demanding two-million credits for some 'vital' information."

"That's not what I wrote and you know it."

"But that's what's written here, Mr. Edson."

And it probably was, Colby knew. It would be nothing for his team to change the message.

"You're not the only one to see the real one I sent."

"Oh, you mean dear Erin? Yes, she saw it, but she's had a medical emergency. Stroke, you know. She's in the hospital now, and it's touch-and-go, poor thing."

You son-of-a-bitch. If my implant was online I'd be beaming this entire conversation far and wide.

And with that thought, all the pieces clicked into place. Why the vice-minister was on the shuttle, why he'd come before anyone else. Why his implant was offline, for that matter. He hadn't believed Colby's message, and because of that, New Mars had been devastated. His negligence had led to the loss of thousands of lives. Greenstein was covering his ass!

"Lieutenant Colonel Sifuentes sent a report out, too. And you can't do anything about that."

"And why would I?" the vice-minister said, his tone oozing corruption. "The colonel and his Marines fought bravely after you smuggled the plant army to New Mars, wrecking your carefully laid plans to take over the planet and all its vital manufacturing."

"So, what is it, Greenstein? I'm manipulating stocks or conquering planets? You're just throwing shit up against the wall to see what sticks."

The vice-minister's eyes narrowed a fraction, and Colby knew he'd drawn blood. Greenstein had come to cover his tracks, but it was a weak strategy and lacked any supporting tactics. The man was trying to wing it, and he didn't have a firm plan yet that would pass the sniff test.

"I'm not the one in the shit, Edson," he said with cold certainty. "You can be assured of that."

Colby recognized the tone, the confidence of the criminally clueless. Given an opening, he'd be able to use that to bring the asshole down. Not for the first time he wondered how Greenstein had risen so high.

The vice-minister prattled on, "You had a good thing going, you know? A fourth star, a cushy life after retirement. But no. You had to go sticking your nose into where it didn't belong. You had to go all white knight, ready for the joust. But you forgot this very vital fact. Sometimes, knights tilt at windmills, things beyond their control."

Colby stopped short of rolling his eyes at the mangled metaphor. As if Greenstein had ever read Don Quixote. Likely he'd seen some watered down Hollbolly vid that missed the whole point.

"Whatever happens to you, remember, it was your choice."

Finally, the vice-minister must have tired of hearing his own voice. He stood up, and without saying another word, let himself out. A few minutes later, one of the guards came back with a bottle of water. He had a black eye, courtesy of Colby and their little fight.

"Captain Heuhn says you deserve humane treatment, even if you are a traitor. I'm supposed to stay here while you drink, so no funny stuff, OK?"

"Scout's honor," Colby said, mentally shaking his head at the young guard's naiveté.

A real soldier would not trust an enemy.

The irony was, Colby wouldn't try anything. His word was good. Maybe the guard wasn't so naïve after all.

The guard unlocked the cuffs, let Colby work some blood back into his hands, then handed him the water. He stood on the balls of his feet, ready to react, but at least he hadn't drawn his weapon.

Colby drained the bottle, then held it at his waist and asked, "May I?"

The guard nodded, and Colby filled it while the guard watched. He didn't care about that. He was a field Marine, and when nature called, there was no such thing as polite modesty.

He shook his hands out one more time, then put them back behind the chair. The guard reattached the cuffs, picked up the full bottle, and left. As Colby settled in, trying to get comfortable, he realized that there was some give in the cuffs.

He pulled at them, and his right hand started to slide. His hopes jumped. The young kid had made a cardinal sin—he hadn't checked to make sure the cuffs were secure.

Colby pulled, almost tearing the skin off his wrist and hand, but after five minutes of tugging, his hand popped free. He stood up, cuffs dangling from his left hand. Ignoring the pain in his right, he swung the cuffs around a few times. They didn't have much weight, but they'd make a passable weapon.

Creeping, he approached the door. He couldn't hear anything on the other side. He leaned forward, pressing his ear against it to hear better, and the door moved. He jumped back, stunned. It had opened a crack. They hadn't even locked it.

He put his hands against the door, ready to give it a shove and jump whoever was out there when sanity caught up with him.

Capital guards were not Marines, but they weren't totally unprofessional in what they did. Even a young guard would not make the mistake with the cuffs, and they would not have left the door unlocked.

He tip-toed back to the chair and took a seat.

The vice-minister had the upper hand, but no matter what the bastard did, Colby could—and would—fight. And no matter how well-crafted the story the vice-minister concocted, some people would believe Colby. All it took was for the vice-minister and his minions to slip up once, and their carefully crafted story would start to unravel.

A traitor who was killed trying to escape, however, could not proclaim his innocence.

Colby sat back and waited for the next move.

****

The door crashed open, jerking Colby awake. He jumped up, holding his left hand back and ready to use his cuffs as a weapon. Two Marines rushed in, then hesitated when they saw the wild-eyed man standing in front of them.

"Not a grateful way to greet your rescuers, General," Lieutenant Colonel Sifuentes said as he entered the room. "Are you going to take us all on with those cuffs?"

"Manny Sif, I'd never would have guessed that I'd ever say this, but you are a sight for sore eyes," Colby said as he lowered his arm. "I take it you are the cavalry, but how did you get Greestein to agree?"

"He didn't. The Commandant insisted that you be released, the First Minister objected, and those two are fighting about it now. I told Greenstein that in the meantime, I was taking you into custody until they could get it straightened out back on Earth."

"And he agreed?"

"I've got over 300 Marines. He's got four SUTAs."

Colby nodded his understanding. Might makes right—and this time, in his favor.

Still, he was in debt to the colonel. Sure, he held the practical power right now, but when everything was sorted out, if Greenstein somehow swayed the first minister and triumphed in the end, Manny Sif's career was over.

Colby felt the lump growing in this throat. This is what he'd missed most after being cashiered from the Corps: the loyalty and bond all Marines had for each other.

Lieutenant Colonel Sifuentes made a show of looking around the room, then said, "Unless you are really attached to these accommodations, General, I'd suggest we diddiho out of here before a firm decision on your status comes down from on high."

He left unsaid the fact that he'd have a much harder time breaking him out if the director general came down on the side of the first minister. It would be better for both of them if Colby was out of Greenstein's reach before and if that was the decision.

And that decision wouldn't necessarily be based on the facts of the matter. Neither the commandant nor the first minister knew the truth. The first minister was backing his Number 2, and the commandant was taking issue with any former general, even a shit-canned general, being held by one of the ministries, even if that was the First Ministry and the minister technically outranked him.

Colby held out his left arm, from which the cuffs still dangled. One of the two enlisted Marines stepped forward, took out his multitool, and a moment later, the cuffs dropped to the deck. Colby rubbed his wrist, and then followed the two Marines out of the door where ten more Marines waited, not exactly guarding two SUTAs, but making no effort to hide that they were waiting for anything.

The guard with the black eye stood casually, thumb stroking the butt of his sidearm as he watched Colby emerge. Colby could see the animosity the young man held for him, and he probably wished he'd just shot Colby earlier, then dragged him out to stage an escape.

You can't hesitate, son, not if you want things to go your way.

Colby gave the young SUTA a huge smile, then nodded his head. The guard's eyes tightened, and for a moment, Colby wondered if he'd be foolish enough to draw his weapon.

Leave him alone, Edson. He undoubtedly believes I'm a traitor, fed by Greenstein's bullshit.

He shifted his gaze and walked alongside the colonel, flanked by the Marine squad, and left the ruined building. He felt a wave of relief as he passed through the shattered door that almost made his knees buckle. Inside his makeshift cell, he'd kept his spirits up by vowing to fight, but as the sunlight hit his face, he realized how deep into the shit he'd been. Without Manny Sif's intervention, he may have not even lived to see another day.

"Are you ready for an update, sir?" the colonel asked as they made their way through the ruined square where the giant daikaiju, including the one Colby had controlled, had fought to the death just two days before.

Colby immediately said yes, slipping back into general-mode before remembering he was no longer on active duty and really had no "need to know," as the military termed it. Still, if the colonel was willing to brief him, he would sure as shit listen. Manny Sif was a heck of a Marine, but he was still just a lieutenant colonel, and this was some pretty heady stuff going on. If Colby could give him any advice based on his years of service, then he owed it to the younger Marine.

"I sent off a cargo pod with what I could scrape up of the different plant soldiers to Lanie Wasserman right after the battle. Lanie is a research fellow at GSI. We were classmates at Command and Staff."

"A civilian?" Colby asked, surprised.

"I had to do something quickly. The plant material was disintegrating as we collected it. We froze some and vac-packed the rest.

"GSI is contracted to the Second Ministry, and Lanie's got clearance. But I routed it through an Academy classmate who's in MCRDD, and he sent it on, cc'ing the chief of staff."

Colby nodded. Yes, that would work. With Manny Sif's chain of command wiped out by the plant soldiers, he couldn't send it up the chain, and the Marine Corps Research and Development Division would be a logical alternate destination. Keeping Lieutenant General Godfrey, the current chief of staff, in the loop covered Manny's ass while getting the samples into someone's hands. They wouldn't stay within the military's control forever, but with Greenstein and his shenanigans, Colby was glad the samples were in military hands for now and not in the civilian side of the ministry.

"Get this, sir. We've already got the initial results. Whatever those plants were, they did not have terrestrial DNA. They are alien."

Which was no surprise to Colby. He'd fought the damned things, he'd been one of the damned things. He knew whatever primordial ooze had spawned them had not originated on Earth.

"Interesting, but why do I get the idea that this isn't the main thing you want to tell me?"

"Because it isn't, sir," the colonel said, looking around at the Marines accompanying them. "We do have a DNA match. Well, not a complete match, but type-match, is what the message said. The DNA is from the Alpha-Nine class of lifeforms.

From the way Manny Siff had said "Alpha-Nine," it was clear the colonel expected him to recognize the designation. If his implant hadn't been offline, Colby would have run a simple search. Instead he had to dredge his memory. He had a vague recollection from some report that had crossed his desk decades earlier.

Alien life had been found throughout human space, something like 43 different types. Most were various types of microorganisms, but a good 15 or so were multicellular. Colby was a Marine, though, and not a xenobiologist, and while he remembered enough to recognize what the colonel was talking about, the specifics were lost to him.

"I'm sorry, Manny, but I'm not up on alien life. What is significant about the Alpha-Nine class?"

"That's what was originally on your planet. I mean your new planet. Vasquez!"

His hair stood on end for a moment, and he wasn't sure why. He'd known that there had been alien life on Vasquez before it had been terraformed, and it still existed in parts of the planet where humans had not yet tilled the soil for terrestrial crops.

Were the plant soldiers native to Vasquez? he wondered. No, Vasquez had been cultivated for nigh on 40 years. We would have seen giant broccoli soldiers before now.

"Anywhere else?" he asked. "Aren't there some classes that are found on multiple worlds?"

"That's the thing, sir," the colonel said, lowering his voice even more. "It's the same class as on fourteen known planets."

"And let me guess, all in the Eidleman Quadrant?"

"Yes, sir. All in the Eidleman Quadrant."

Vasquez was on the outskirts of human space, pushing outward in the Orion Arm. Most of the human diaspora was inwards, toward the galactic center where more densely packed solar systems offered a greater chance of finding Goldilocks planets to settle or terraform. But that didn't mean space beyond Vasquez was empty. With over a billion stars in the Orion Arm, there were still hundreds of millions of stars out beyond his adopted home, hundreds of millions of stars that could harbor an untold multitude of lifeforms.

Something tickled the back of his mind, almost like the touch of his implant when he was taking control of the plant soldiers. A need to expand, to find a new. . . garden? What if the boss plant wasn't an invader, but a defender? Hell, what if its troops weren't actually soldiers? He'd spent most of his life in the military, so it only made sense that he'd interpret the situation from that perspective. But he'd been a farmer these last years, and from that point of view the boss plant wasn't an adversary, it was just. . . a gardener! Panic started to bubble up, and he physically shook his head to clear it, pushing uncomfortable thoughts deep to where they couldn't surface.

". . . Sixth Ministry has already gotten wind of it and are demanding access," Manny was going on.

Colby focused on the here and now.

"Sixth Ministry? They're the science arm of the government, so that makes sense," he said, acting like he'd heard everything the colonel had just said.

And they don't have the power to do much else, he thought, still concerned about his own future.

The huge organism that was the government would be shifting to take over the situation. An alien invasion had been the fodder of the media since the 20th Century, and every agency had to have contingency plans ready for this. It wasn't up to Colby to play hero anymore, so his thoughts went to self-preservation. And as he'd learned when he fought corruption before, that might be difficult to attain. With the military under the control of the First Ministry, there wasn't much even the commandant could do if the first minister wanted his scalp.

****

Lieutenant Colonel Sifuentes handed Colby a readout. He gave it a quick read, then crumbled it up and tossed it to a trash can, bouncing it off the rim and to the floor of the Marine's CP.

"He won't quit, will he?" Colby said in disgust.

It had been a copy of yet another message to the first minister, demanding that Colby, Manny, and all the Marines on New Mars be arrested for traitorous actions against the Republic. Clearly, Greenstein was in panic mode.

Was he even aware of how ridiculous he sounded? Did he seriously expect that anyone would authorize the arrest of 300-plus Marines? And not just any Marines, but the very same Marines whom he'd already lauded for turning back the plant-soldiers attack. But the man was a politician, first and foremost. He didn't have to make sense. The rest of the Marines were just bargaining chips in a larger game. Greenstein wanted his ass, and now probably Manny Sif's as well. He likely thought that if he could yell loud enough and long enough, it was possible that the commandant would concede, just to shut him up, and in the process give up the two of them.

"You know, you didn't have to make a target of yourself. You didn't have to take action on my part, Manny."

The younger Marine looked up at Colby, and his eyes hardened for a moment. "With all due respect, General, I am rather insulted that you would even voice something like that. You're a Marine, an honorable man despite what happened, and Greenstein is scum. There was no other choice, sir."

Dutifully chastised, Colby nodded. He'd been wrong. Manny had acted on his honor.

Still, he was very grateful for it.

"OK, then," he said, anxious to change the subject, "where do we stand with the power grid? Is there anything I can do to help there?"

"Not unless you have a G-39 in your backpack, General. Until we get the Corps of Engineers in here, I'm afraid that power is going to be—" he started before he went glassy-eyed in the manner of a person getting messages over his implant.

Colby automatically queried his before remembering he was cut offline.

The colonel listened for a full minute before he snapped back and shouted out, "Sergeant N'belle, get the major over here ASAP and put the battalion on Deployment Alert Bravo."

He got to his feet, and Colby asked, "Can you tell me what's happening?"

"Oh, of course, sorry, sir. That was the commandant herself. It seems as if she and the Chief of Naval Operations took notice of our reports, and they're not waiting for the first minister or the director to get off their collective asses.

"The RS Pattani, a corvette, and a packet destroyer have just entered New Mars orbit. Our orders are to lead a mission back to Vasquez, retrieve any survivors, and assess the situation. If there are still enemy there, we're to engage them. But our prime mission is to keep any more of them from getting to New Mars. Up to and including, if necessary, destroying the wormhole from the Vasquez side."

Colby felt the familiar surge that accompanied the call to battle, and jumped to his feet, anxious to return to action. It took a conscious effort to calm back down. This wasn't his fight anymore.

"And Greenstein?" he asked. "Are they coming to arrest him?"

"Greenstein? No, unfortunately. The commandant said to treat him with kid gloves for now. Politics, you know."

And the commandant still doesn't know which way the wind is blowing, he thought bitterly.

Which wasn't fair. General Piper Nilson bled Marine Corps green. She was from the Basic Officers Class just after Colby's, and she'd been nothing but professional since then. If she ordered Greenstein to be treated with kid gloves, then she had a good reason for that. Which didn't mean the asshole wouldn't eventually get his just desserts somewhere down the line.

"What Marines are on the ships?" Colby asked. "Are you still in command?"

The Pattani, as a frigate, had a minimal crew and normally no Marines on board, but between the three ships, they could carry up to a battalion-minus of Marines or a mix of special operation-types. That would probably mean a full bird colonel in charge.

"Sir?" Manny asked, looking perplexed.

"Are there other Marines in the task force? And are you still in command?"

"You didn't . . . wait one, sir." He went glassy-eyes again, and Colby could see his throat moving as he sub-vocalized.

He turned back to Colby a long minute later and said, "Sir, G-8 is . . . well, hacking the block on your implant. The commandant is confident that they'll get it back online with all its previous functions reactivated. That's probably going to take a few hours, but the paper pushers will need that long to go through all the protocols anyway."

"Protocols? Why?"

"With all due respect, General, I should think that would be obvious. Your commission is being reactivated. You're in command." "With all due respect, General, I should think that would be obvious. Your commission is being reactivated. You're in command."

Interlude I: Adjusting for the Impossible

By the time the destruction ceased, the Gardener had completed the regrowth of a minimal body sufficient to its need. The new form secured its enhanced cranium in a snug space beneath the rubble of what had once been one of the structures so prized by this brand of Meat. There was adequate airflow to bring it information, enough moisture to suit its current requirements. From its dwindling supply of resources it had generated and repurposed data collectors into sentries and scattered them around its location. It was safe, for the moment, or at least as safe as any Gardener enduring such circumstances might manage.

Reality, such as it was, could no longer be trusted. Although it had never itself indulged, the Gardner possessed knowledge of a variety of potent alkaloids capable of altering one's brain chemistry. Profound and disturbing hallucinations might be achieved, or, with the right combinations, schisms and even complete breaks from reality were possible.

It found the concept offensive. Trained in design and empiricism, it struggled even to entertain the thought experiment that reality could be subjective. It was nonsense. One could not design a garden, let alone the landscape of an entire world, without an unwavering appreciation for and understanding of objective reality. One gardened by obtaining a mastery of the interplay of complex but predictable patterns. A garden did not spontaneously reject its nature. Grassland did not transform overnight into forest, mosses did not become ferns, conifers did not choose to change themselves into liverworts. Reality operated by rules, laws that could be deduced and observed. It was vast but fixed.

Except no one had bothered to inform the Meat, not here on this world of mud and Mech, nor back on the planet that it had intended as its latest garden. The purge agents it had unleashed on this world should have overcome local resistance. This was an established fact. Yet, somehow, they had been destroyed down to the last leaf.

No matter. The mega seeds it had planted had been hard-coded at a genetic level to possess sufficient response patterns to defeat any assortment of Mech or Meat in the known galaxy. For them to do otherwise was as inconceivable as rain falling upward to fill the sky with clouds. But again, reality, as it appeared to be defined in this place, among these Meat, had proved otherwise.

No Gardener felt threatened by any configuration of Mech. At worst, they were an inconvenience and short-sighted, hasty. No Gardener feared Meat, even more ephemeral and chaotic. Nuisances, nothing more. And while this Gardener had been surprised by the antithesis of Meat wielding Mech—Meat that had learned to overcome its native gravity well and venture into space, infesting other worlds, other systems, with filth and sprawl and thanatopic entropy—still it had expected to overcome the creatures readily enough.

The Gardener had not imagined that the same Meat that had obtained a modicum of mastery over Mech would somehow merge with its own much more sophisticated vegetable systems. But this Meat had. This Meat had commandeered its vessel. This Meat had compromised its purge agents. This Meat had even launched its own mega seed and, not content with that gross deed, had used its own paltry consciousness to override the mega-seed's behavioral programming and subvert the mighty structure to its own heinous purposes. □

Reality should not allow even the possibility of such a synthesis of Meat and Mech and Veg. Had not, in all the time since the primal flash. Until now.

If reality, as it understood it, no longer held sway, if order had surrendered to chaos in less time than the simplest of seeds might germinate, the empiricism demanded that this Gardner must embrace chaos.

But only in a very orderly manner, flush with internal consistencies born out by direct observation, repetition, and revision. □

Several rotations of this muddy and underdeveloped world occurred while it grappled with these fundamental changes. During that time the lifeless pieces of its purge agents had broken down beyond the cellular level. This had been part of their reality, to return to the soil, to be carried away upon the air, to circulate in the water upon whatever planet they were unleashed. The trio of shattered hulks constructed on the□templates of its mega seeds had similarly begun to decompose. Even the usurped creation of this Meat had begun to give way to the natural process. Entropy will out.

In this new unreality, pursuing its own version of synthesis was not the answer, would not defeat the blend of processes this Meat had employed. No, the Gardener resolved to maintain its integrity of vision. It would not taint itself. But chaos did require sacrifice. Purity would be lost. It could not stand apart from what this Meat had done, not if it had any hope of restoring reality and then warning its fellow Gardeners. It would have to blend as well, remain itself, separate but no longer apart. Only through thorough empiricism would it find the means to defeat such repugnant chaos. Only by learning from this Meat could it achieve a state where all such knowledge might be stricken from the galaxy.

It had expanded its ratiocination to its theoretical limits and examined the situation from every angle, every perspective, evaluating each and every known and unknown, selecting from the resulting options and scenarios until it had found one that offered the most promising outcome. And then it had begun allowing its massive brain to decay. Soon after, the rest of its body began to follow suit. Little time remained to this form.

The particulate remnants of all its creations, even the recent data-gathering sentries, hung in the air. It required little effort to produce a pollen that altered these bits into the iota of a vast network. As the pollen spread, the network expanded throughout the air in all directions. And as the Gardner itself came apart, it distributed its intellect and sense of self to this network. The near infinite scintilla of itself, endless, nearly invisible specks of green, smaller than the smallest of spores, in time landed upon and adhered to every surface of Meat and Mech, and continued to spread further, carried by its unwitting hosts. □

In this form, conscious but bodiless, the Gardner would wait, would observe, and when it had gathered the critical data that would yield its success, it would strike. □

And the Meat—despite its mastery of Mech or its recent impertinent synthesis with Veg— being clueless Meat, would succumb, likely without any awareness of how much trouble it had caused or how it had summoned its own eradication.

Part II: Thorns, Weeds, and Roses

"Did you think you could hide from me, Edson?" The sneer in Greenstein's voice grated on Colby's nerves.

Colby turned away from Wendi Utica, Manny Sif's logistics officer, and said, "Excuse me, Captain."

The task force had received a warning order to be ready to deploy back to Vasquez, and even with only a single, understrengthed battalion, there were a million moving parts that had to be coordinated.

Kid gloves, Edson, kid gloves, he repeated the mantra in an attempt to be civil to the vice-minister. He looked up at Greenstein, a half-smile on his face.

It didn't work.

"Captain, where is your commanding officer?" the vice-minister demanded from Utica.

"Colonel Sifuentes? I think he's in the armory, sir," she answered automatically before her face fell, and she looked at Colby, asking, "I mean, if that's OK for me to say that."

"Why do you want to know, Vice-Minister?" Colby asked, almost choking on his words.

Greenstein stared at Colby, then turned his body so that there was no doubt that he was snubbing him, and said, "If your commander isn't here, then I order you to arrest this man."

"Sir?" Captain Utica asked, clearly confused.

"Did I stutter? I told you to arrest this man. He was in my custody until some . . . people in military uniforms . . . released him. Those people will be found and prosecuted, but as I know your name, Captain. . ." he said, turning to look at her name tape.

Captain Utica kept turning away from him, keeping her name tape from his sight, and he almost chased around until with a shout of victory, said, "Utica!

"As I know your name, Captain Utica, it won't be hard for me to find you if you do not obey my orders. So, get your Marines and arrest this man now!"

She looked up at Colby, clearly out of her depth, then said, "I . . . I can't, sir."

"What do you mean, you can't? Can't or won't? I'm warning you, your career is about to come to a very unpleasant end."

"She can't, Vice-Minister. You have no authority to give her any such orders."

Greenstein had been deliberately ignoring Colby, but at this, he turned towards him, his face turning red as he almost choked before managing to get out, "What the hell do you mean, Edson? I have the authority, and you damn well know it."

"In that, you are sadly mistaken," Colby said, a smile forming despite his half-ass attempt to control it. "You do not have the authority."

Greenstein stared at him, mouth gaping open. He turned to look at the two of his capital guards as if for support. The SUTAs glanced about at the eight other Marines in the room, Marines who were taking an intense interest in what was going on. Greenstein's guards evidently decided that discretion was the better part of valor because they failed to look the vice-minister in the eyes. They might be jerks, but that didn't mean they were stupid.

Even without their moral support, the vice-minister did not back down. Instead, he ramped up the rhetoric, pitching his voice as if surrounded by media recording him for the evening news, and addressed everyone around him.

"I am First Ministry Vice-Minister Asahi Greenstein. I have declared Colby Edson in violation of Civil Code 1402.3b. As such, it is within my authority to request assistance from any Republic constabulary or federal troops to carry out arrests and detainment," he said before breaking down into normal speech, "That means you Marines. You have to arrest Edson."

Captain Utica had regained her composure. She stepped around Edson and said, "If the general were a civilian, you could charge him with whatever that code is. But since he is a Marine, all charges have to be referred through the Commandant of the Marine Corps via SJA-1."

"Edson? A general? He used to be a general, Captain, but he got cashiered," Greenstein said, the gloat in his voice almost enough to make

Colby step up and punch him. "Now he's nothing but a farmer at the ass-end of the galaxy."

Four of the Marines stepped forward at his words, and the two SUTAs instinctively took a step closer together. Colby held out his hand, palm outward, to stop the Marines.

Before he could have the satisfaction of giving the vice-minister the news, Captain Utica said, "He may be a farmer, sir, but he's also an active duty lieutenant general of Marines."

Once again, Greenstein looked poleaxed. This time, Colby didn't hold back the grin.

"That's correct, Vice-Minister Greenstein. As of . . ." he said before checking the time, ". . . eight hours and thirty-two minutes ago, I've been recalled to active duty. Sign, sealed and delivered."

"But . . . but you were cashiered. You were kicked out for cause."

"You're never completely out, vice-minister. You're simply transferred to the inactive list, there to be recalled at the whim of the director."

"She signed off on this?" he said, a note of panic in his voice.

Colby could practically see the wheels turning in Greenstein's mind. If the director had signed off on Colby's reactivation, then that could portend a new political wind, and ever the politician, he was acutely aware of how things could change.

"As I said, signed, sealed, and delivered."

The vice-minister stood there silently for along moment, and Colby could almost hear the gears spinning furiously in the man's head.

"I'm going to want this confirmed, Edson—"

"General Edson."

The vice-minster almost snarled, but said, "General Edson. I want to speak with the commandant. I assume you realize that as a vice-minister, I have the authority to dema . . . to request that?"

"Of course, sir." He turned to the captain and said, "Please relay the vice-minister."

"I'd be happy to, sir," she said with sarcastic enthusiasm.

As a civilian, even a high-ranking civilian in the First Ministry, Greenstein did not have a military implant. His commercial implant could connect him throughout human space, but only through the commercial relays. The main relay on New Mars had been turned into so much rubble by the alien daikaiju, so to call back to Earth, he either had to use his ship's comms and then request a patch to the military side of the ministry, or he could be patched right to HQMC via Captain Utica's.

"Sir, code two-three-bravo-niner-six-foxtrot-zero-four-four," the captain said.

"Thank you, Captain," Greenstein said as he flipped down his earset.

He turned away as he started sub-vocalizing, not that Colby could have picked up what he was saying even if he tried. The reason he'd had the captain relay Greentein's call was that his implant was still offline. Now, if he'd had it, as a Level 6 implant, he could listen in.

Captain Utica caught his eye and raised her eyebrows. She could listen in without too much trouble. Colby shook his head, suddenly feeling guilty for his own thoughts along those lines.

The vice-minister was getting angry, pacing back and forth, punching the air with his right hand in a fist. That made Colby happy. The guy should be rotting away in a federal cell, preferably on some planet with heavy gravity and noxious air, but for now, no matter how petty it might be, Colby was enjoying this.

Until the vice-minister suddenly stood up straight, his right hand raised to his ear. He nodded, then said aloud, "So, I am the senior First Ministry rep?" He nodded a few times, then said, "Thank you, General McTimmons. I'll pass on to the first minister how cooperative you've been."

Colby's stomach gave a lurch. General McTimmons was the Assistant Commandant of the Marine Corps, who, along with the two force commanders, was on an equal level as a vice-minister. And if Greenstein was happy with whatever the ACMC had just said, Colby was pretty sure he was going to hate it.

"Thank you, Captain," Greenstein said in a saccharine voice. "You've been a great help."

He turned to Colby but made a show of stowing his earset, keeping him waiting.

"Well, General, it seems that you have been reactivated after all. Congratulations are in order, I guess. We'll worry about the charges after this operation back to Vasquez is over."

Colby waited for the other shoe to drop as the vice-minister looked at him with triumph gleaming in his eyes.

"Is that all?" Colby finally said, losing the battle of wills.

"Oh, no, now that you mention it. It seems that I've been made the senior First Ministry rep for the mission—you know, to make sure this thing is actually done correctly. And as you are part of the First Ministry, and, of course, as I out-rank you, I am in command."

Colby stared at the vice-minister in shock.

He's in command? Of a military operation?

"I'm going back to my ship, General. I'll expect a full brief in . . . oh, let's give you time to get this done . . . in two hours?"

With that, he wheeled around, snapped his fingers at the two Capital Guards—who seemed more than eager to leave—and marched back out of the room. As soon as the hatch closed behind him, Marines broke out into questions.

Colby started to activate his implant before he remembered he was still cut off.

"Quiet!" he shouted before turning to the captain and saying, "Get to the ACMC's office and find out just what is going on."

Colby had felt like taking a victory lap only ten minutes ago, but victory had been snatched right out from under him. If Dickhead was right, this mission had just turned to shit.

****

"General, the vice-minister wants to inspect all the Marines," Major Nkundlande-Siphers passed. "What do I tell him?"

"Excuse me, Captain," Colby said, holding up a hand. "I need to handle something."

Greenstein was being a pain in the ass, but it hadn't been as bad as he'd feared. First, he was not in command of the task force, as much as he wanted to believe it. Task Force Roundup was a military operation, pure and simple, and Colby was in command. Still, the first call he'd received once his implant had been reactivated—the Marines hadn't been able to hack it yet, but as part of the compromise with the civilian side of the First Ministry, the block had simply been turned off—had been from the commandant himself. He told Colby to humor Greenstein for the moment. Colby had objected, wanting to arrest the man, but what had been simply a request from the commandant immediately became an order that brooked no argument, and Colby immediately shut up about it.

The vice-minister had cancelled the brief he'd told Colby to give him (which was just one less possible confrontation as Colby had planned on sending a junior officer to do that). He'd stayed in his ship, emerging once the Navy arrived and again just now. He'd spent five minutes making sure the Navy knew he was in charge, and now, eight hours later, he'd come out again with his latest demand.

Colby knew the man was just trying to let everyone know he was in charge. It was petty, but Colby could play the game, too.

With his implant back to its full capability, he didn't have to subvocalize. Years of experience enabled him to "think" his messages, and the implant sent them.

"Take a squad from Alpha, have them lay out their full gear in component mode, weapons disassembled. Give him a checklist, then we'll see how long he lasts."

"Oh, sir, with all due respect, you are a cruel man," the major said.

"How do you think I got three stars, my young major. Edson out."

Marines absolutely hated a component inspection, referred to as "junk on the bunk." It was onerous to set up and easy to fail. With so many parts, it was almost impossible to have them all in perfect condition. What the junior Marines didn't necessarily realize is that the SNCOs or officers conducting the inspection hated them even more, if that was possible.

"I'm sorry about that," Colby told the Marines and sailors in the small, almost-intact room he'd commandeered as his CP. "Captain, you were saying?"

Captain Alicia Whitehorse was the composite fleet commander as well as commanding officer of the RS Pattani, a Naha-class frigate and the designated flagship of the task force.

Colby had not been familiar with her, which was not surprising. She'd just made captain, and he'd been out of circulation for awhile. A quick scan showed that she was an up-and-comer, one of the Navy's brightest stars. Highly experienced and decorated, Colby was glad that it had been the Pattani that was close enough to answer the call.

It wasn't that the other two captains and ships were lightweights. Commander Deshal Brockmorton of the corvette RS Portnoy Bay, and Commander Nick Pierce of the packet destroyer RS Gazelle had excellent records as well—no one got command of a Navy ship without being one of the best—but Whitehorse and the Pattani were one-percenters.

With the ongoing crisis with the Borealis Pact, Colby was surprised that the Navy had even sprung the three ships. It was necessary, as the plants represented a clear and present threat to humanity, but the plants were an unknown to the command while they understood the very real danger of the Borealis Pact.

"Yes, General," the captain said. "There was some talk about waiting for the Surrey County to arrive so you could have assault craft for your Marines, but based on your initial report, the sector commander thought time was of the essence."

The RS Surrey County was a Ground Assault Carrier, designed to forcefully insert Marines on an enemy-held planet or moon. Vasquez might still be technically enemy-held, but Colby didn't think that the Surrey County's capabilities would be needed to land his Marines.

The sector commander had been right, time was critical. Topeka and Riordan were still there, and Riordan needed medical care. Chances were that more survivors were on the planet as well who'd managed to hide or run, and while Marines could stand up to the plant soldiers, he knew civilians couldn't face them head on and survive.

"The Pattani has more than enough spaces for your Marines, and with our ship's shuttles and my gig, we can land you in two waves. With your warning order, we've tentatively chosen two locations, here and here," she said, waving her wand. Vasquez appeared over the table, then the image zoomed in to DeStaffney Station, where Colby, Topeka, and Duke had battled the plant soldiers and found the enemy ship, then it rotated to Tennison, the second collection point for the planet's agricultural products.

"Once you debark, we will take the guard position at the wormhole while the Portnoy Bay and Gazelle remain on call for any support you need."

The image of Vasquez disappeared, to be replaced by images of both of the smaller ships, along with their armaments. As always, Colby was somewhat in awe of the power even a smaller capital ship had. A corvette was a pirate and smuggler hunter, and the packet destroyer was a ship killer, but either one of them had more firepower than a regiment of Marines. He was confident that if his Marines needed fire support, either ship would be more than capable to supply it.

Neither ship could touch the firepower of a frigate, however.

"Explain to me one more time why the Pattani is going to remain by the wormhole and not in orbit."

Colby had received the ship disposition already, and even as the task force commander, there wasn't much he could do to change it, but he wasn't quite sure of the whys and wherefores as of yet.

"If we have to destroy the wormhole, sir, then the Pattani is the only ship of the three of us capable of doing that."

Destroy the wormhole? Then Vaquez would be isolated. Why? he started to wonder before it hit him. *Of course. We killed the plant boss here on New Mars, but if a new one can. . . sprout?. . . then we cannot risk it getting through here, and then to other systems.*

"And why only the Pattani?"

"Neither of the other two ships have a Pluvian Doomfist. The Pattani does. Imploding a wormhole is, well, it's a balancing act between brute power and a delicate touch. The ship has to be in the exact center of the wormhole, and you know how they keep shifting with gravitational fluxes. Then, the PD has to be set for a close-sphere field induction. And trust me, General, if the induction fails to spark full pluviation, imploding the wormhole will be the least of your problems. We're talking a wave of quantum instability spreading out from both ends.

Colby couldn't understand half of what the captain was saying, but he nodded sagely.

"And that will destroy the wormhole?"

"If we keep the induction field at max output for between 20 and 30 seconds, yes, sir, it should."

"That can't be good for the ship and crew."

The captain laughed, then said, "No, sir. It won't. We'll get the crew off on the life-capsules, but the ship itself will be lost."

Colby knew how captains felt about their ships, and he was surprised that she was so matter-of-fact about the potential for her ship to be destroyed. He decided right then and there that not only did Captain Whitehorse have a sterling record, but he rather liked her. She was the kind of warrior he understood. She was his kind of people. The kind of officer who would unflinchingly sacrifice her own career much as he had done. He hadn't met many in his long career, and stumbling over one in the current situation struck him as an omen of sorts.

Well, Edson, that means you need to make damn sure she doesn't end up sacrificing herself to close that wormhole. What a waste that would be.

"And the Surrey County? Does this have the Puluvian . . . Ploovi . . . uh . . . the same capability?"

"No, sir. None of the amphibs have the PD. Frigates and battleships, and only the newer ones at that."

It was just as well, Colby thought. Ever since humans left their caves to fight one another, those in charge always wanted more firepower, it didn't matter if it was bigger clubs or bigger spaceships, that need had never changed. He didn't have to like it, but Colby knew that when the time came, he would make full use of whatever they had.

"Well, let's hope it never comes to that," Colby said. "So, what are we looking at for leaving orbit?"

"We're ready when you are, sir."

"Colonel Sifuentes?"

"Without the armor, we're light. Top Wunton's already aboard the Pattani doing a quick embark brief, but we'd be ready to load out in 30 minutes."

The armor was a sore spot. It had proven extremely effective against the plant soldiers, but somehow, they'd almost all been disabled, gummed up, and CWO4 Mikhailov, the battalion armorer, had said that some components couldn't be repaired. With 331 Marines, the task force had exactly five working sets of battle armor.

"We always say that it's the Marine who're the dangerous weapons, not what we arm them with, so this might be the time to prove it."

Colby watched his officers. Manny's attempt to suppress a grin was less successful than Whitehorse's effort not to roll her eyes. "Let's start the embark. I want every ass-slap onboard in ninety minutes. Can we do that?"

Even with a diminished battalion of only 331 Marines, that was asking a lot, but as a commander, he knew when to push.

Manny Sif looked to Captain Walsh, his S4, who gave the slightest of nods in return.

"Yes, sir, we can."

"Then let's do it. Captain Whitehorse, Colonel Sifuentes, I would like to see you and your principle staff on board as soon as we depart the system."

Colby didn't need his implant to know they were both relaying instructions down the lines of their respective chains of command.

"Are we all good?"

"Yes, sir," came the chorus of the gathered staff.

Colby stood up, signaling the end to the meeting, and the Marines rushed out, leaving the space to Colby and the sailors. Colby shook the hands with each of the Navy officers and the command master chief before they left.

Better get yourself ready, too, Edson.

He hadn't even been issued a weapon yet. Time to find Mikhailov and rectify that situation.

He'd taken only two steps when he felt the telltale ping and his implant took an incoming call from Major Nkundlande-Siphers.

Hell, what does Dickhead want now? he wondered before accepting the call.

"You were right, sir," the XO said. "Greenstein only made it through half of Corporal Mont Arif's inspection before he gave up. Told me to finish it."

That's not even as long as I figured.

"Doesn't surprise me. We're embarking now, though, and you've got the vice-minister watch. Go tell him to get to the shuttlepad."

"He thinks he's taking his little Markus X, sir."

"Last I heard, a Markus X's a luxury corporate ship, not a military man-of-war. If he wants to come, he'll join us on the Pattani."

"Uh. . . sir. No disrespect intended, but I don't think he's going to listen to me. He still thinks he's in command here."

Damn, Edson. You can't delegate every interaction with that bastard.

"You're right, Major. Let me handle di. . . with the vice-minister. You've got more on your plate that you need to deal with now."

Generals normally didn't worry themselves with the details of getting individuals aboard ships, but this was a unique situation. Besides, the more he thought about it, the more he knew he was going to enjoy telling the vice-minister that he couldn't take his fancy ride to Vasquez.

****

"Any signs of life?" Colby asked. "Human life?"

The last two hours on and then in orbit around New Mars had been hectic, a case of controlled chaos as the Marines embarked aboard the Pattani. He'd had one last meeting with the Navy and Marine Corps staffs, but once they left orbit and headed to the Vasquez wormhole, the Navy took over, leaving Colby alone with his thoughts.

Those thoughts veered into territory he'd just as soon avoid, but once started, they wouldn't let go. He'd left Topeka and Riordan on the planet when he'd commandeered the alien ship to get back to New Mars, and he couldn't help but feel that he'd abandoned them. The planet hadn't been secured from the alien threat, and for all he knew, the plants could have sprouted up armies of the daikaiju since he left.

"Not much, sir," the sailor on the bioscans said. "I count just four-hundred and thirty-three humans."

"Four-hundred thirty-three?" Colby asked.

"That's all. Sorry, sir."

Vasquez had been a highly automated colony, and prior to the invasion, there had only been just over 2000 inhabitants on the entire planet. Sixteen hundred people killed was horrid enough, but over four hundred survivors was more than he could have hoped for.

"And at DeStaffney Station?" he asked.

"I've got forty-one, sir."

That doesn't mean Topeka made it, but if there were that many people there, he'd bet she was already in charge of them. He felt a load lift off his shoulders.

"Sir, do we proceed?" Manny Sif asked.

"Nothing else out of the ordinary?" Colby asked the rest of the Navy CCC crew.

The holovids showed Navy captains battling aliens from ships' bridges, looking out through vast windows into space. There was nothing like that in actuality aboard a Navy ship. The Pattani was controlled from the CCC, the Combat Command Center, located deep in the center of the ship and heavily shielded from enemy attack.

All 15 of the scantechs shook their heads. Colby realized that none of the ships extensive scanners was set up to identify specific plant life, but several systems would notice 30-meter tall plants roaming the landscape, and with 433 humans still alive, the planet had to be relatively secure.

"Captain Whitehorse, are we ready?"

Her eyes lost focus for a moment in the manner of someone on her implant, then she was back, giving Colby a thumbs up and saying, "Shuttles and the gig are up and ready."

"Very well. In that case, Colonel Sifuentes, let's launch."

He gave a quick order to his implant, and a moment later, a dedicated circuit was created, linking him directly to Captain Whitehorse.

"I'd like you to keep this circuit open," he passed. "Just in case."

If she was surprised at his voice suddenly sounding in her implant, she didn't give any hint of that. She nodded once, then passed, "Will do, sir."

"Well, you keep the Navy ready up here in case we need a ride off Vasquez."

"Aye-aye, sir," she passed as he turned to make his way to the hangar deck. "Go with God, sir."

Colby stopped and slowly turned around, a smile on his face, before uttering the standard response, "Don't need God for this. I've got my Marines."

****

Duke gave a yelp of joy as the captain's gig hatch started to open and Vasquez air flooded inside. She broke past the Marines and bolted over the half-opened hatch to the sunshine, jumping around like a puppy.

I know what you mean, old girl, he thought as he started to push forward.

"Sir, you need to wait until we clear the area," Sergeant Dela Cruz told him, his voice grave with the heavy responsibility of making sure nothing happened to him.

Colby wanted to order him to stand down—Manny Sif, who'd landed in the first wave up at Tennison, had already reported no sign of vegetable combatants, only some very relieved civilians, happy to see the Marines. It had been bad enough acceding to the lieutenant colonel's insistence that he wait until the second wave, but to have a Marine squad, led by someone who looked like he should still be in secondary school, was very frustrating. He wasn't an invalid, and he could still fight the fight, if it came to that.

And, surprisingly, he was excited to get home. Yes, "home." He'd only been on the planet three years since his exile, but he'd gotten used to the pristine air and pace of life. He could see Duke cavorting around, stopping to roll in the dirt, and he wanted to get out of the gig and feel Vasquez's sun on his face again.

He couldn't do that to the sergeant and his squad, however. The young Marine was taking his mission seriously, and even a general had to bow to how the Marines conducted things.

He waited as the hatch fully opened and Sergeant Dela Cruz gave his orders to his squad. The Marines rushed out, weapons at the ready while Colby cooled his jets, still watching the deliriously happy Duke cavort before she suddenly looked up and bolted out of his view. He was just about to ask the sergeant what was going on when the Marine returned to the open hatch and said he could come out.

With a little more emotion than he'd have thought, he stepped out of the hatch and onto Vasquez soil, the good loamy aroma reminding him of just what made the planet such a perfect place to grow crops. A better place couldn't have been created by all the agritechs in humankind. He almost knelt to touch the soil, to test if it was about ready for pyro berries.

Come on, Colby. You're not a farmer anymore. You're a Marine again, and you don't need to be checking out soil conditions.

He raised his gaze from the soil and toward the station, where Duke was attacking one of about 40 civilians who were being held back by a fire team of Marines.

What the . . . he started to wonder before it came into focus. Duke was lunging at a familiar person's face, to be sure, but to lick, not rend.

Colby strode across the field, two fire teams of Marines forming a wedge around him. Hopeful faces watched him approach, only a few he recognized. Lassie Heldreman ran a farm with her son Jack about 20 klicks farther from the station than his, and he'd helped them erect a new silo. He scanned the others, but he didn't see Jack, which might account for the look of sorrow on her face. There was Father Demopoulos, the defrocked Orthodox priest with whom Colby had bartered snap beans for a decent wine. David and Jia Li Manus, with little Foster grasping his mother's hand, stood smiling hopefully at him. He saw Lazer Montgomery, one of the planet's four equipment techs, someone who'd probably visited most of the people on the planet at one time or another.

He didn't recognize most of the others, which gave him pause. There hadn't been many people on the planet to begin with, and he'd must have been living like a hermit not to know them.

But there was one other familiar face, and Duke was right there, her tail whipping back and forth.

"Took you long enough, Edson," Topeka Watanabe said, her hand patting Duke's head.

****

"Well, he's full of himself," Topeka remarked.

"I call him Dickhead," Colby said, as the vice-minister walked away after making sure he told the gathered civilians that not only was he in charge, but he'd ordered this mission to rescue them and they owed their very lives to him.

"Dickhead? Why General, I'm shocked and befluttered that you would stoop to such gutter language, and around my delicate sensitivities at that," she said in a highly affected voice.

"You don't know him like I do," he said, unable to keep the bitterness out of his voice.

That took the smile off her face, and she said, "I think there's more to the story here than meets the eyes, and you've got a history with him."

"You could say that," Colby said, leaving it at that.

He was not going to get into how it had been Greenstein who'd railroaded and got him kicked out of the Corps and exiled to Vasquez in the first place. That was too close to the bone, something that was personal. Somehow, some way, he was going to make sure that the vice-minister paid for his sins—not for screwing him over, but for the corruption that Colby uncovered that had led to Greenstein taking him out first.

"Well, if I wasn't such a lady, I'd say that if that motherfucker messed with you, then I'll be glad to kick his fucking balls so far up his ass he'll need a mining permit to find them."

Colby looked at Topeka first in shock, then in relief as he laughed out loud. At first glance, she looked innocent, a petite young woman with the face of an angel. By now Colby knew she was a kick-ass terror who would make a sailor blush with her language.

Whether she meant to or not, she reminded Colby to get to the task at hand, not worry about some pissant vice-minister whose days were numbered—hopefully, that is. Even that bastard couldn't pull enough strings to cover his ass over ignoring the plant invasion after being warned about it.

Then again, he got away with stealing from the Corps.

He shook off that line of thought and said, "OK, you were telling me about the new growth."

"Yes, sir," Fiorio Slavas, a hop-bean farmer from the Thames Creek area, said. "The first plant-things, they stripped my fields bare, you know. Like what you said happened to you down here station-way. We barely got out ourselves, with those things chasing us until we got on the outcropping."

Colby had never met Fiorio until 30 minutes ago, and he'd never known that north of DeStaffney Station, the terrain was dotted with close to 50 rock outcroppings that sprung out of the otherwise flat ground like kopjes.

"Me and Leda," he said, nodding to a florid-but-smiling-faced woman who was looking on with interest, "we stayed up there for two days. We could see the smoke and all from station-way, but we didn't know what was happening. Finally, we came down, 'cause we were mighty hungry, you know like.

"We went back to the farm to see what we could scrounge up, and our fields, they were covered."

"Tell him how fast, Fiorio," Leda said.

"I'm getting to that. Like Leda says, these weren't no sprouts or nothing. They was like two meters high."

"Three," Leda said.

"Three meters high," he corrected himself. "Only they weren't nothing from Earth, that I can tell you. I didn't want to touch them, so we left to come to the station here."

"And what did we see?" Leda prompted him.

He looked a little puzzled, then said, "The station all destroyed like this?"

Leda rolled her eyes, then stepped in front of her husband, saying, "What he means is that while we were walking here, there were kilometers of the alien plant forms. They'd taken over the entire terrain. What had been a nice big pine forest was gone, an alien horticulture in its place, but one far more developed than our own terraforming could do in thirty years."

Colby mentally counted out the days since the attack. It had been less than a week, either five or six days. His trip to New Mars and back had screwed up his calendar somewhat.

He looked to Topeka who nodded and said, "It's like that all around here. Big swathes of land have been repopulated with non-native plants."

Well, all of our crops and plants are non-native. We introduced them here, he thought, but kept that to himself.

"Hold on a second," he said, raising his hand, palm out.

"Manny, I'm getting reports that new vegetation is taking over large areas here, supplanting Earth-vegetation. Is it the same thing up there around Tennison?" he asked over his link.

"Wait one and I'll find out," the lieutenant colonel passed back.

"And none of the new plants attacked you?" Colby asked Leda, ignoring her husband.

Several voices broke out, too many to hear what was being said, and Colby had to hold up a hand again to shut them all up.

"Leda, if you please."

"None of them pursued us, if that's what you mean, and some of them, you could touch without anything happening. But others, some of the smaller ones, the ones with the shiny trefoil leaves, they're like guards. Touch them and you'll regret it."

"They burn!" David Manus said, holding up an arm with a wicked-looking red blotch that ran from his wrist to his elbow. "I barely got away with my life."

"All hands, avoid contact with any shiny plants with trefoil leaves," he passed to the Marines while he listened.

The entire force had been ordered not to come into contact with any non-Earth vegetation, but this little tidbit deserved greater dissemination.

"Did they chase you?" Colby asked David. "After you got burned."

"We were coming in to the station with Kob 'Mbelle," he said quietly. "I got burned, he started swinging a scythe he'd managed to make. We ran," he said, pointing at Jia Li and Foster. "Kob stayed to fight, and they swarmed him."

"There was nothing we could do," he said, his eyes pleading for Colby to agree, to release the burden he'd been carrying.

Maybe David could have pulled Kob away, maybe he couldn't. That was not for Colby to say, but he did understand the guilt. Every commander who'd sent men and women to die in battle had felt the same thing.

"You had to take care of Foster," he said.

He didn't expect David to accept that, and from his expression, he hadn't. He'd have to deal with that demon himself.

"So, if you attack them, they will attack back. But they won't hunt out people and chase them down?"

"Not that we know," Topeka said.

"I'd like to see some of these," Colby said as Sergeant Dela Cruz came alert. "Can you show me?"

"There's some not too far," one of the women he didn't know said. "I can show you."

"Sir—" the sergeant started before Colby cut him off.

"Don't worry Sergeant. You're coming with me. And we're just going to see them, not touch them."

"General, what's going to happen to us?" someone else asked as he started off to see these guard plants.

I guess I never told them that. Of course, they want to know.

"For now, we need you all to hold tight. We'll bring down some more supplies, but the first thing we need to do is to make sure the planet is secure. Once we've done that, the republic will send in a liner. All of you who want to leave will be taken to New Mars for transit onward."

"But you said New Mars was hit, too," someone shouted out.

"Only Hellasland was hit, so the rest of the planet is functioning. Besides, our wormhole only leads there, so that's the only way out from here.

"I should also say that there will probably be a significant monetary incentive to stay here on Vasquez. That's far above my pay-grade, so I don't know the details. but the Republic wants the crops we've grown here."

"I hope they like alien crops," someone muttered as Colby turned to go see the guard plants.

They'd only gone a hundred meters when Major Nkundlande-Siphers came running up to them.

"What, Sergeant, did you rat me out?" Colby asked.

He knew the Marines thought he had to have protection, but this was getting ridiculous. He came to a stop and waited for the major, ready to cut the man off.

"General, I didn't want to pass this over the net. But you know that plant-boss thing?"

"Yeah," he answered, a sudden hollowness forming in the pit of his stomach.

"From how you described it, I think it's back. First platoon saw it, or another one just like it, running away from the captain's gig and into the trees. A couple of the Marines fired on it, but they think it got away."

"How did they miss?" Colby asked, his voice a little too strident.

"They were at the station, sir. There wasn't an obvious reason to put a guard on the gig."

Which was true, Colby knew. But that left an opening, that left hope.

"So, the gig is 500 meters from the station?"

With the station landing pad torn up and covered with debris, the shuttles and gig had landed in an open field outside of the rubble.

"Yes, sir, about that."

"So, they might have been too far to see clearly?"

"Two meters tall, broccoli-looking thing that moved along a bunch of roots?"

Whatever hope he'd been grasping at was gone. He looked to Topeka who had a resigned look in her face.

"The Gardener's back," he said.

Interlude II: Passage and Illumination

Boarding the Meat vessels had been simplicity itself. Its consciousness was borne upon uncounted numbers of specks carried aboard each of three craft in the days before departure. Greater numbers of specks were left behind on the planet itself, but the Gardener simply withdrew its awareness from them, passing those portions along to bits upon the vessels. Initially, once it understood that the trio of arriving vessels would soon depart, the Gardener had considered maintaining its consciousness upon all three. It abandoned that strategy when it became clear that the Meat that had interfered with its garden on the earlier world would be leaving as well and traveling aboard a specific craft. That Meat had stolen its vessel, co-opted its purge agents, imposed its will upon a mega seed. None of its fleshy associates had given any indication of such capabilities. Obviously then, the greatest opportunity to nullify this species involved marshaling its powers in proximity to the only Meat that had demonstrated any intelligence beyond the simple destruction that defined all of them.

Much as it had withdrawn its awareness from the specks scattered outside of the three vessels, the Gardener abandoned its presence on the other craft and consolidated its intellect and cognition aboard the vessel that would transport the Meat it now considered its only real opposition. Once that had been accomplished, it applied itself to a better understanding of the Meat, the better to eradicate the pest from its garden and, potentially, the rest of space.

Gardeners did not measure time in the frenetic way of Meat. Time was subjective, different for different things. The life cycle of growth, the seasons of a world, the movements of planets, the generations of limbs and roots within every different plant and tree and shrub. None of these were the same, not like the units of seconds and minutes that so entranced these Meat, defining their lives at every step. The Gardener balanced both forms of perception. The rotations of this world, prior to the vessel's departure, contained both a billion Meat busy moments but also, for it, only a single contemplative point, even given its consciousness distributed across so many specks throughout the Meat vessel. Each speck observed, recorded, sorted the data presented through its limited sensorium. Each passed every datum forward to be collated and compared and considered by the gestalt of all. The data flow might be vast, but it hadn't yet yielded true knowledge. Nor had the Gardener expected it to; little learning occurred at the level of the microscopic specks.

Exceptions existed. It only required the loss of several tens of thousands of specks to the vessel's crude atmospheric filtration systems before the Gardener's consciousness learned of the brutal assault on so many of its components and steered its elements away from the numerous passive intake valves found in every space aboard.

In counterpoint, it also identified numerous, out of the way nooks where it could gather and reproduce its constituent numbers to more than make up for the losses from the vessel's systems. Moreover, as small, clumpy layers of green accrued on the underside of consoles, along containers in seemingly locked storage areas, and throughout the exterior lengths of conduits hidden from regular view, the Gardener generated nodes of concentration and processed the massive influx of information. It came to understand, to its astonishment, the nature of this variety of Meat.

They engaged in meaningful, complex behaviors that resembled true language. Many forms of Meat in the Gardener's experience made use of audible signals for basic communication, but these had been limited to Call systems, finite subsets of content limited to informing others of danger, the presence of food, or sexual availability. But this form of Meat actually spoke to one another. The language was crude, to be sure, but also open-ended.

Once the Gardener had realized they had language, it discovered something equally astonishing. They had not inherited the Mech at their disposal, they had created it themselves.

However unthinkable, the parsing of their newly acquired language as well as the trickle of details from its countless observers left no doubt. This Meat had developed and designed the means to remove itself from its planet of origin and was well on its way to infesting large swaths of the galaxy. Moreover, they had discovered a technology that its own people had missed. Gardeners understood how to fold space, from the edge of one solar system to the edge of the next, eliminating the need to traverse the empty space between. This Meat lacked that ability but instead had harnessed portals that traversed space of orders of magnitude greater. But typical of Meat, they did not truly understand what they did, could not control it, and used it only opportunistically.

Thus had they left the worlds of their infection far behind when they discovered its garden and bespoiled it for their own purposes. That passage had presumably skipped over vast regions of space, systems where other Gardners toiled for their art or nurtured the seeds of society's successive generations, each side utterly unaware of the other. Cluelessly, the Meat had reached beyond the safe range of worlds unknown by Gardeners and intruded where they did not belong.

All this it had learned and one thing more. The specific Meat of its attention on this vessel, and the other two craft besides, were returning, back through the far-from-understood portal. All unknowingly, they would be taking it back, back to a region of space it understood, back where it had resources scattered in caches across the planet from its seeding two hundred cycles before. Regardless of its own fate, in less than a rotation upon that world, it could encode everything it had learned into messenger probes to be sent on to its people. This rabid and uncontrolled Meat required action, preparations for defense, contemplations for its eradication, likely even a long-range plan to identify, locate, and purge the hundreds of worlds it had already infected. It was. . . ambitious, the kind of plan that would require incalculable spans of time. But then, what was time to a Gardener?

Part III: Pyrrhic Melons

"We need to track it down, Captain. Period."

"Yes, sir. We'll do our best."

"No, you won't, Captain," he snapped. "Your best isn't good enough. You'll get it done. Am I understood?"

"Yes, sir. We'll do it."

Colby looked at the crude sketch of the area drawn by one of the survivors. The Gardener had been spotted running into the small pine forest on the far side of the captain's gig, the same one where it had landed its spacecraft during the initial invasion.

It's not staying there—it's only passing through the Earth trees. It wants its own kind, he realized, "because it's not behaving tactically. It's not some kind of vegetable soldier, it's a Gardener!

"Captain, change of plans."

"Sir?" Captain Wallace Singh asked, clearly confused.

Be clear, Edson. That's on you.

"Your mission is still to kill the boss plant, but it's not in the pines."

"Where is it, sir?"

"Leda, come look at this," he said, calling the woman over. "This area right here is the pines over there," he said, pointing. "And over here, this is how you came to the station, right?"

"Uh, yes, I think so," she said, her eyebrows scrunched up as she tried to make sense of the sketch.

It's not that hard. This is just a map. Look at it, he thought, before he realized he was being too demanding. Calm down Edson and give her a break. She's never seen a printed map, much less one hand-drawn from memory before.

"Look, your home is up here. You walked down this road, so you must have passed the area on the other side of the pines, right."

She pulled it closer, and after a moment, Colby could see the understanding flood her face.

"Yes. Yes, we came that way."

"OK, you told me that most of the area had been taken over by the alien plants, right? So, are there alien plants on the other side of the pines?"

She studied the map as if she could see the answer in the drawing, before she said, "Yes. They were the alien plants. I'm sure of it."

He thanked her, then turned back to the patiently waiting company commander, saying, "OK, Captain, I don't think the plant boss is in the pines. I'm betting it'll be over here. I want you to go around the pines at the double time, then look for signs of its passage."

He considered having the captain try and surround it, but the area was just too big. No, his best bet would be to run the thing down, like Early Man running down a gazelle.

"And I'm coming with you," he blurted out before thinking.

"Sir?" the captain asked.

Two minutes before, he'd told the captain that he'd be staying at what was left of the station to coordinate the two landing areas, and now he'd changed that, too. The man had to be wondering if Colby had lost his mind, but his training kept any such thoughts off his face.

"I'm coming with you. I've had more experience with this thing than anyone else."

Beside him, Sergeant Dela Cruz stepped up, a protest forming on his lips, but Colby stopped the Marine short with, "And you're coming, too."

"And don't forget me," Topeka said quietly—but leaving no doubt that she was not asking permission.

"Fine," he said, not wanting to argue.

Within two minutes, Captain Singh was moving his company—minus a squad that was left with the civilians—out. Colby and Topeka were in the rear of the formation, surrounded by not only Sergeant Dela Cruz's team, but two squads from Singh's company. They'd only gone about 20 meters when Duke broke free of the man Colby had asked to hold her and streaked through the Marines to him.

He just accepted her presence, reaching down to pat her head just before the company broke into the double time. Topeka grimaced, but she kept up.

Colby had led the way five days prior when he and Topeka had run to the Gardener's ship, and he'd been the one pushing the pace. That was then, and this was now. Surrounded by fit, young Marines, Colby was feeling his age in comparison as they jogged to go around the pine forest. He kept his face steady, smiling and nodding at the Marines who kept looking at him, but inside, his gut was in spasms, and his lungs cried out for air. He was glad when they got off of the natural ground and onto the hard road that led north out of the station. He was still sucking wind, but at least the footing was easier.

Beside him, Topeka was in worse shape, but she struggled ahead. At least Duke wasn't having any problem, darting back and forth between the Marines and Colby.

Within a klick, they rounded the pines and started the gentle downslope into the bottomlands. Going downhill was easier on the lungs, but it changed his stride. Beside him, Topeka was struggling, and he thought she was going to stop until a Marine stepped up, told her to grab the back of his assault pack, and dragged her along.

She looked mortified as Colby caught her eye, but he knew that telling her to go back would be useless. She was seeing this through.

They'd only gone another 800 meters or so when the Marines in front of them slowed to a walk. Like an accordion, the formation collapsed on itself, and Colby stumbled, running up the back of the Marine in front of him.

"You OK, sir?" the Marine asked, turning around.

"Fine, son. No problem," he said, keeping his voice calm despite his burning lungs and trembling legs.

All senior Marines, officer or enlisted, thought that they were the same private or lieutenant who'd first joined the Corps. It was hard to accept that bodies aged, let alone admit it. Several of the younger Marines were breathing hard, but Colby was not going to show he was suffering even if it killed him.

He was tempted to query Captain Singh about what was going on—more than tempted. But he held back, slowly trying to recover his breath. And then, they rounded the last bend in the road, the entire bottomlands stretched out before them. In the far distance, he could see the tops of the Hastert Hills through the light haze.

Just 200 meters ahead of them, the agricultural richness of the bottomlands began, and the lead platoon was deploying from a column to a line, getting ready to enter the nearest field.

"This was Megan Tines's farm," Topeka said quietly between deep breaths as they looked out over the bottomland.

Colby had never met the famous Megan Tines, one of the first farmers to receive a charter on the planet, and one of the most successful. She'd grown the delicate vacuberries, a good money crop that Colby wouldn't have attempted on his farm until he had far more experience.

What had been acres of the low vacuberry vines had now been replaced with large, round, vaguely melon-looking things—two-meter-tall melons. They were a bluish-green, evenly spaced, each one about four meters from the next. Between them were smaller plants. The transformation had taken only days.

Something about the larger plants bothered him, like an itch he couldn't scratch, but for the life of him, he couldn't put his finger on the reason.

"Has anyone reported seeing those, yet?" he asked Topeka.

"Nothing like that."

"Take a full bio scan of the field 70 meters to my zero-two-zero," Colby passed to the watch officer on the Pattani. "Let me know what they show."

"Roger that, sir."

Colby didn't know what had sparked that thought, but sometimes, a commander had to go with his gut. If nothing else, this would be just more data for the science-types back on Earth to pore over.

Without an immediate threat to the wormhole, Captain Whitehouse had switched rolls with the Pattani in geosynchronous orbit over DeStaffney Station, and the other two ships doing a detailed ground scan of the planet.

Ahead of him, the first platoon was about to enter the field. Colby watched nervously, taking a couple of steps forward. Sergeant Dela Cruz and Private Queen, a huge, 130kg Marine, matched him, step-by-step.

OK, OK, Sergeant. Don't get excited. I'll be a good boy and stay back.

He could monitor the company net, though. With a brief mental command, he was listening in to the Marines.

"We've got movement," a Marine—Colby's implant identified him as Lance Corporal Morganstein—said.

Colby ordered a direct feed from the Marine, and he could see what looked to be several meter-high plants moving forward. They weren't the trefoil type, but there was a sense of purpose to their movement.

Stupid feed. Why isn't it clearer? he fumed, trying to determine what was about to happen.

Only the feed was normal, he realized. It just didn't compare to the immersion he'd experienced back on New Mars, when he was "seeing" through the plant soldiers.

The cracka-cracka of a burst of automatic fire reached him, and Colby pulled back from Morganstein's feed. More Marines started firing. Colby resisted the urge to run forward and take over, but he'd learned long ago that would be an invitation to disaster. Generals could set the stage for their Marines, but when it got down to brass tacks, it was up to those same Marines to fight the fight. Trying to get involved would only confuse matters, and that would get Marines killed.

He flipped from the orbital feed to the captain's and then to his own eyeballs, settling on the latter. The Marines, some 15 meters deep into the plants, were being attacked by the smaller, one-meter-tall plants. The big melons remained motionless. Hundreds, if not thousands, of the smaller plants were swarming the Marines, who were retreating in good order, firing into the mass. There were too many for the slug-throwers to cut down, so the Marines had switched to their

M88s. A fine green mist rose up between the rows of melons. Waves of plants were exploding into bursts of green goo as the water in their bodies was excited to a boil by the beam weapons.

Not all, though. Colby saw one Marine, then another, then three more fall beneath the onslaught. If the plant soldiers had been able to tear a Marine in a battlesuit apart, Colby knew these Marines stood no chance.

"Sir, we have to retreat," Sergeant Dela Cruz said, pulling on his arm.

Colby whipped the arm free. He wasn't going anywhere while the Marines were in contact.

If the Marines had retreated pell mell, then more would have fallen, but their disciplined retreat, with each Marine's fire supporting the other, kept most of them alive as they emerged from the field. Orders were flying over the net, but Colby kept quiet, letting the NCOs fight the battle. And he was proud of what he saw. He knew how terrifying the plant soldiers could be, things out of nightmares, but the Marines never faltered.

The plants did, however, much to Colby's surprise. They stopped at the edge of the field, green arms waving, but not moving forward even as more fell to the Marine fire.

"Cease fire, cease fire!" Marines shouted, passing on the order as they stopped 20 meters away and faced the plants. Colby could see NCOs checking their Marines.

"General Edson, what are your orders? Do you still want us to advance?" Captain Singh asked him over the person-to-person net.

Colby stayed silent for a moment, trying to get his thoughts in line. Something told him that the Gardener was out there among the melons and small soldiers. If nothing else, the fact that the small soldiers had stopped at the edge of the field was indicative that they were being controlled.

"No, stand ready for the moment," he ordered the company commander.

He switched the link and called Captain Whitehorse. "Captain, can you drop the hammer on the alien lifeforms at these coordinates?" he asked blinking in and uploading them. "I'd like it with one fell swoop."

"Let me check, sir. Wait one."

"What are they doing?" Topeka asked.

Colby shook his head, reaching one hand down mindlessly to pat Duke's head.

"General, the disposition of the alien plants is haphazard, so our GIP Cannons would require multiple salvos. Additionally, you and your Marines are too close. You'd have to retreat back a minimum of 500 meters.

Crap.

If the Gardener was in there, he wanted it trapped. If the Pattani had to fire in salvos, that would give the boss plant warning, and it could slip away during the bombardment.

Wait, can't they adjust their beam cannons?

"What about your . . ." Colby started before he had to query his implant to see what the Pattani carried. ". . . your BTY-1210. Can't you start that in a circle, then focus it in on itself?"

"With Betty? That's affirmative."

"Great! And is that danger close? I mean, do we have to move back first?"

"No, sir. It's focused finer than a gnat's ass. You won't be touched."

"OK, then I want you to encompass the entire growth here. Burn the native . . . I mean the Earth crops as well, but I want this entire field eradicated. Nothing escapes, understand?"

"Got it, sir. I'm passing this to Guns now."

"Guns" was Lieutenant Commander Tannibeth Rystal, the ship's weapons officer.

"I want that in 60 seconds Captain."

"Uh . . . no can do, sir."

"What? Why not?"

"We've got the ship-to-ship lens on Betty now. We need to change that out."

Colby wanted to lash out. In typical Navy fashion, the Pattani had its most powerful weapon in ship-to-ship mode, leaving the rest for ground support. The Gardener hadn't shown signs of naval warfare, and as it turned out, the ground-and-pound guns were not suitable for this mission.

"How much time do you need," he asked, fighting to keep his voice calm.

"Twenty minutes, maybe less."

"Make it fifteen."

He cut the connection, scanning the field with his naked eyes. Fifteen minutes seemed like forever, and he had visions of the Gardener slipping away before the Pattani could fire.

"Captain Singh, stand by. We're going to ash the plants in fifteen. As soon the Pattani stops firing, I want your company in there. If there's a speck of green left, burn it."

"Roger that. No problem."

Colby told Topeka what was going to happen, then checked in with Manny Sif. Manny reported huge swathes of alien life, but none of the melon pods. Three Marines had been burned by plants, but none of the plant soldiers had actively attacked them.

It was only here, between the hop-bean farms and DeStaffney Station that the plants went into attack mode. That had to signify something— just what, he didn't know.

"Give me a countdown," he told Captain Whitehorse needlessly.

"Roger that," she said, probably wishing he'd stay out of her knickers.

OK, that's the last time I ask.

Nine minutes later, he asked how much longer it would be.

"Look at that," Topeka said before the captain could answer.

In unison, like a sped-up version of sunflowers following the track of the sun, the melons moved to "aim," for lack of a better word, at the eastern sky.

"Captain Singh, get ready!"

But the captain had already acted. The Marines aimed their weapons, ready to take on whatever came their way.

"Captain Whitehorse, we need your Betty now!" he passed to the Pattani's commanding officer.

Several things happened at once. The small soldier plants, the ones that had attacked the Marines, seemed to collapse. The nearest line of melon pods twisted to orient on the Marines, and the rest shot up into the air, like watermelon seeds squeezed between two fingers.

"Fire!" he shouted at the Marines, taking over the company net.

The first salvo let loose just as the nearest line of melons . . . spurted . . . a greenish-yellow mist.

"Nose filters!" rang out over the net from a dozen voices as the mist flowed toward the Marines, engulfing them in seconds. Nose filters or not, the Marines started to stumble and fall as Colby shouted out for the platoon around him to fall back.

It was useless. The mist rolled over them, and Marines began to tumble. Topeka, too. Colby held his breath for as long as he could, running to get out of the mist, Duke on his heels. Finally, he had to breathe, and he knew he'd be taken down, too. He gulped in the air . . . and nothing happened. There was a minty taste to his mouth, but he was fully functional. As was Duke, who sat and looked up at him, head cocked to one side.

All around them humans were on the ground. Only the two of them were upright. There had to be a reason for that, but he didn't have time to figure it out. Most of the melons had taken off.

"Captain Whitehorse, we've had a launching. Burn everything leaving the planet."

"We see it, General. There are over a thousand of them all broadcasting signals similar to the telemetry recorded from the alien ship you commandeered."

"Just burn them, Captain," he roared aloud.

"We can't, General. We just got the ground lens on. Betty is no longer configured for ship-to-ship. We're engaging with all other weapons systems and missiles now, and I've called back the Portnoy Bay and the Gazelle."

"Get them all. Not one escapes."

"Sir, there are thousands, and they're tiny. I . . . I'm not sure we can. Sorry to cut you off, sir. I've got a fight on my hands."

The captain cut the connection. She knew her duty. They couldn't allow any of the melon pods to escape.

She'd have made a helluva Marine.

He looked around. Marines were on the ground around him. His heart rose to his throat as he dropped to his knees next to a Marine, a lance corporal with "Kukuro" on his name tag. The Marine's eyes were open, and Colby could see the fear in his eyes.

He's alive, at least.

"Lance Corporal Kukuro, can you hear me?" he asked.

The Marine didn't respond, but there was something in his eyes that lent belief that he was conscious.

"If you can hear me, roll your eyes."

Was there the tiniest bit of movement there? That might be wishful thinking, but something told Colby that the Marine was alive. He looked around. All of the Marines he could see had open eyes.

There was nothing he could do for the hundred-plus humans at the moment, so he marched down to Mz. Tine's farm. The front row of pods, the ones that had spit the green mist at him, had collapsed upon themselves and hung limply among the small dead soldiers. Colby gingerly stepped between two of the pods, stamping on the plant soldiers. Beyond that front rank, the pods had all gone, leaving a base of leaves that were wilting as he watched.

"General Edson," Captain Whitehorse passed on the net.

"What is it? Have you stopped them?"

"Negative, sir. We've downed a couple hundred, but there're too many. And there's no doubt about it. They're heading for the wormhole."

Shit, shit shit!

"See what you can do, Captain. Get as many of them as you can."

"You know I can't do that, sir. You know I have my orders."

"But . . . but, that means . . ."

"That's why we get paid the big credits, sir. We'll do our duty. Commander Brockmorton will take over and pursue all the surviving pods."

There was nothing else he could say. Their orders were clear.

"It's been an honor, Captain, a true honor."

"Likewise, sir, likewise. Well, if you'll excuse me, I've got quite a bit on my plate at the moment.

The connection was cut as Captain Alicia Whitehorse maneuvered the Pattani to enter, but not pass, the wormhole.

"Commander Brockmorton--" Colby started to pass.

"I've got it, sir. We're chasing the pods, but their awfully small and agile."

"No matter where they go, you're not to give up, understand?"

"Roger that, sir."

Colby felt defeated, and he shook his head. Duke whined beside him.

"Why us, girl? Why are we still standing?"

Because we've got some of the plant in us now. We're connected. We've both been touched by the damned things.

For a moment he wondered if he was being controlled somehow, and that scared him. But he felt like Colby. He thought he was still himself, still Colby.

As his gazed wandered, he realized that there was one pod still upright.

Malfunction? he idly wondered.

He wandered over to it, hoping to gain an insight that would help the two remaining ships destroy them. As he approached, the pod split open from top to bottom. Colby stepped back, and pulled his sidearm out of his holster, suddenly feeling vulnerable.

Like a baby passing the birthcanal, the Gardener emerged, looking much like it had in the moment before Topeka had cut off its head. Duke erupted into a flurry of barks and lunged at it before Colby could grab her.

Instead of attacking, the Gardener knelt, one of its leafy hands outstretched to the dog. Duke stopped, whined, then leaned forward, her nose almost touching the thing. Suddenly she wagged her tail and licked the arm.

Colby was flabbergasted. What had just happened?

His implant activated as if receiving a call, but it wasn't from Captain Whitehorse or one of the other two ships. He wasn't sure what it was for a moment as the transmission swept back and forth as if trying to find the right frequency. He almost understood something a few times, but then it was gone, leaving a trace of familiarity.

Realization hit him. It was the Gardener.

"What do you want?" he sent to it.

Maybe it took both of them sending, because almost immediately, the Gardener's thoughts filled his senses.

«*Extraordinary Meat. Meat with language. Meat with the trappings of Mech. Meat in space, on other worlds, on this world. My world. Short-lived, arrogant meat. This world was barren thousands of cycles past. Barren until I arrived. I seeded its oceans with plankton to change the atmosphere. I introduced fungi to change the surface of the land. I set these in motion to to do my work and went away. I returned two hundred cycles past, and as I intended this world was ripe for planting, for the garden I had planned. It was majestic, exquisite, but still so young. I fine-tuned the design, adjusted the ecosystems I'd spawned, and went away again.*

And then you, arrogant foolish Meat arrived. You ignored what your own senses told you, and sought to undo all my efforts.»

Colby had already suspected this, he realized. He just hadn't wanted to admit it, that it might be humans who had been the aggressors here.

«Meat destroys. It always has. Your own history acknowledges this, though you choose not to apply this truth to your own species. You despoil everything you touch. You will go. You will take these others with you and leave my world so that I may restore this garden.»

"But it doesn't have to be this way. We didn't know you were here. Hell, we didn't know you existed. There has to be another way here, one that does not result in death and destruction."

The Gardener seemed to dismiss the concept, but there was something, a hint, a germ, that Colby picked up. The possibility intrigued the boss plant. He tried to formulate another tack when a voice shouting "Edson! My God, where are you?" reached him.

What the hell is he doing here?

"I see you, Edson, I see you!" Vice-Minister Greenstein shouted out even louder as he daintily picked his way through prone Marines, arms held high as if to avoid contact with them.

He pushed into the field and approached Colby.

If you want to knock out my Marines, why not knock out him, too? he thought at the Gardner.

There was no answer. He received the slightest whiff of curiosity instead.

"My God, Edson, what happened here? Are they dead? And is that the head plant there?"

"They're unconscious—"

"Sir, I'm Vice-Minister Asahi Salinas Greenstein. I'm here as the representative of the Republic. Of all humanity. I am authorized to speak to you in the name of the chairman."

Bullshit. You don't have authorization for anything.

"And let me tell you, my friend," he said, pushing past Colby as Duke gave a low growl. "We have huge potential here. Huge."

Colby wanted to tell Greenstein that the Gardener couldn't understand Standard, but he realized that the bossplant was, not listening per se, but paying attention. Suddenly, he knew that he was playing the part of translator. He heard the vice-minister's words, and the Gardener was picking them through his thoughts.

"I've seen what you've done here, and I'm impressed. Truly impressed. We can take those capabilities and totally revamp the agricultural business. Hell, a backwater dump like Vasquez could supply all the crops needed by humanity, all of them, just using your agritech. We'll be rich, and I mean filthy rich."

Colby was shocked. This was beyond the pale, even from a snake like Greenstein. He wanted to take the man by the throat and shake him like a terrier on a rat, and only the Gardener's presence held his hand.

"How does that sound to you? I mean, you don't need Republic credits, of course, but I can give you whatever you want. Raw materials? Fertilizer? Weapons? You name it, you've got it. My family, we're big in the weapons business, so, I've got the inside track for that.

Colby felt a mental shudder emanate from the Gardener when Greenstein said "weapons." Colby was just disgusted. The man was trying to work a deal here, of all things.

"What about the Marines?" he asked. "Some of them died here."

The vice-minister seemed to remember that Colby was still standing there. He frowned, then waved a hand, saying, "That's why they get hazardous duty pay, Edson. And we can't let past . . . past disagreements get in the way of future cooperation."

He turned back to the Gardener and said, "Speaking of weapons, my family's are top-of-the-line, but your soldiers, they are pretty incredible. We can take that tech and make new weapons, with the best of both civilizations. No one would be able to stop us, and they'll all pay top credit to keep up with the rest who'll buy from us.

"And if someone balks, well, we'll have the weapons, so we can pretty much force them to comply, if you know what I mean."

The Gardener had been standing motionless, but after the last comment, something changed. The plant shuddered, then from out of the mic on Colby's collar, spoke.

«*This is what Meat does. What it seeks. Destruction for its own sake. And being impressive Meat you aspire to ever more impressive forms of death. This one revels in it, crafts personal goals predicated on it. Short-lived Meat, why do you not savor life rather than pursue death? I have no weapons, but I can momentarily repurpose other tools to address your desires.*»

A blast of mint-green mist blew out from the Gardener and enveloped Greenstein. Unlike the Marines and Topeka when their mist had hit them, Greenstein immediately started to convulse. He grabbed for his throat as a pea soup of froth came gushing from his mouth. His terror-filled eyes looked at Colby, and he managed to spit out "Edson!" before he fell to his back and lay still.

"That's General Edson to you, Dickhead."

The Gardener stayed still and silent as if waiting for Colby's reaction. He wasn't so sure his connection with the plant species would help him if the boss plant decided to take him out the same way.

"Beginning final approach into the wormhole, General," Captain Whitehorse sent. "Will initiate pluviation."

"Understood, Captain," Colby said, a lump forming in his throat.

"I'm sending the crew off now. Take care of them, OK, sir?"

"Will do, Captain," he said, then following that a few seconds later with, "You know, you don't have to stay. You can't do anything to help the pluviation team."

"You're wrong there, General. This is my ship and my crew. I can't leave anyone to do this on their own. I'm sure you understand."

"Yes, I do. I wish there was something I could say."

"Just take care of them, Marines and sailors alike. You're going to be cut off from human space. I've got it easy. My job will be done in a few minutes. You've got the tougher task in front of you."

Colby thought of what could have happened. With his commitment to the Corps, and then his banishment, he'd never married. But Alicia Whitehorse, he could see himself with a woman like her, someone he'd admired.

"Go with God," the captain said, just as she'd done two days before.

"I don't need God. I've got the Republic Navy, Captain."

There was a moment of silence over the live connection, then a quiet "Thank you, sir," before it cut off. The net was still live, so the Pattani was still up there, but he knew he'd never hear from her again.

He turned back to the Gardener, angry at the wasted lives. He was pretty sure the thing knew what had just transpired, and it probably knew that Colby was angry. Anger would get them nowhere, though, especially if they were trapped on Vasquez. There might be upwards of 700 humans on the planet and one Gardener, but it had proven just how quickly it could raise a division of fighters.

"This doesn't have to end like this," he said. "Turn your pods away from the wormhole and we'll still have all the same options left to us. No one else has to die. Just turn them around."

«They have no will that might be subverted or persuaded. No sensibility that might be reasoned with. I crafted their purpose and navigation into their very seeds. I can no more change their destiny than you can will your arm to bud new hands all along its length.»

"So, what are you going to do now?" he asked, more to give the Pattani time to complete its mission rather than to hear the answer.

His implant blipped once to inform him the ship had entered the wormhole. Not much longer now.

«I will restore my garden, undo the scars you have wrought and recreate beauty and poetry. And you, the weeds in my garden, will be gone from here. Impressive Meat, flee back through your spacial anomaly. My pods will follow. You have demonstrated that your kind is too dangerous to leave its worlds. My pods will alert others of my kind, summon them with the means to contain you and end your threat.» It paused and Colby felt its attention on Duke for just a moment before it resumed. *«You understand there are higher orders. You are*

Meat that suborns lesser Meat, just as I command all the vegetation of this world. You do this for your own purposes and often to the benefit of that lesser Meat that serves you. You restrict it, instruct it, educate it, to the degree that any of these things are possible for lesser Meat. Such is your future. You will be restricted to your worlds. Space will be denied you, as will the means of transit. You will not be harmed, but you will be contained.»

And that is so much bullshit, Colby thought as he waited for the inevitable. And finally, it happened. The Pattani went off the net. Colby sent a simple query through his implant to . . . nothing. His implant still worked, and it still had terabytes of data, but there was no connection back to humanity. They were truly cut off.

"And now you've lost. That was the Pattani with a handful of brave men and women, destroying the wormhole. You don't know anything about my people, where they are. We're safe from your . . . weeding. Meanwhile, we've got two more ships chasing down whatever of your pods are still out there. They will follow your pods to the ends of the galaxy, if they have to.

«Resourceful Meat, you continue to surprise. I had not imagined your capacity for death included self-destruction if it achieved your ends. But you have failed. My pods don't transition to your area of space. I don't need to create a beacon there for my people to find you. It is enough to inform them of your existence,

your capabilities. Many of the pods that launched seek their way home, and you have only two vessels to pursue. It is a long journey, and you are short-lived. The galaxy is vast, but we are patient. Only one needs to get through. Once they are alerted, informed of your existence and the threat you pose, my people will repurpose themselves to find you.»

While the Gardener pontificated, the Marines around them began to stir. Whatever had knocked them out was short-lived. Colby sensed that the Gardener was about to lash out, probably with its more lethal mist.

"You've lost. It's over. They're going to burn you where you stand, and destroy every atom. There will be no coming back this time."

«I am but a leaf on a tree in a single forest. My own existence is insignificant. The designs I imposed upon this world have already been set back in motion. Strike me down again, perhaps for a final time. It is your way. But it changes nothing. Not upon this world, nor elsewhere.»

"Colby!" a welcomed voice cried out from the edge of the field. He didn't turn around, but he could hear feet pounding. A moment later, Topeka was at his side, staring at the Gardener, the same one she'd beheaded a week before. Marines flowed to either side of him, weapons aimed and waiting for the order to open fire.

He didn't have to. Duke barked twice, and as if that was a signal, the Gardener collapsed, its body decomposing into mulch as they watched.

It was over . . . right?

The melon pods were ships, no doubt about that, and he knew they were being sent out as some sort of spacefaring vegetable message beacons, letting the other gardeners know there was Meat out in the galaxy, Meat that fought back. If the Portnoy Bay and the Gazelle could catch and destroy every one of them, well, all for the good. That would just delay the inevitable confrontation that would eventually happen. But humankind was aware of the gardeners now, and they wouldn't be caught by surprise.

"What now, Colby?" Topeka asked.

There were about 700 people on the planet between civilians, sailors, and Marines. That wasn't much, but it was enough to be a viable population. The planet was fertile, if they could control the gardener's plantings and make sure their own crops thrived.

"Now, we live," he said.

"Really? That's all you have to say?"

He shrugged.

"I guess you're back to being a farmer. And here I was, just getting used to calling you General."

Colby thought about that a moment. He had his Marines, and soon enough he'd also have the surviving sailors from the Pattani, but Vasquez had little need for either.

"You're right," he told her. "Looks like I'll have my hands full teaching a lot of people how to be farmers."

She nodded and said, "I guess I'm going to have to learn to be one too. Not much of a demand for shipping now, is there? Don't suppose you want to teach me?" she asked, looking away from him as she petted Duke on the head.

The dog wagged her tail in pleasure.

He slowly reached out and took her hand.

"Yeah, I'm a farmer again, but at least I've got my commission back.

Schoen and Brazee

Thank you for reading *Bitter Harvest*. We hope you enjoyed it. We welcome your review of our novella on Amazon or any other website.

SEEDS OF WAR
Invasion
Scorched Earth
Bitter Harvest

Other Books by Lawrence M. Schoen

If you would like updates on Lawrence's new books releases, news, or special offers, please consider signing up for his mailing list. Your email will not be sold, rented, or in any other way disseminated. If you are interested, please sign up at the link below:

http://eepurl.com/c7257X

Barsk

Barsk: The Elephants' Graveyard
The Moons of Barsk

The Amazing Conroy
Buffalito Buffet
Calendrical Regression
Barry's Deal
Buffalito Destiny
Trial of the Century
Buffalito Contingency

Selected Short Stories

A Fool's Death
Bidding the Walrus
Pidgin
Mars Needs Baby Seals
The Game of Leaf and Smile
The Moment
Thinking
The Wrestler and the Spear Fisher

Books Edited/Published by Lawrence M. Schoen

Alembical
Alembical 2
Alembical 3
Alembical 4
Cats in Space - Elektra Hammond (ed)
Cucurbital 2
Cucurbital 3
Eyes Like Sky and Coal and Moonlight - Cat Rambo
Rejiggering The Thingamajig And Other Stories -
Eric James Stone
The Wizard of Macatawa and Other Stories - Tom
Doyle

Author Website

http://www.lawrencemschoen.com/

Other Books by Jonathan Brazee

If you would like updates on Jonathan's new books releases, news, or special offers, please consider signing up for his mailing list. Your email will not be sold, rented, or in any other way disseminated. If you are interested, please sign up at the link below:

http://eepurl.com/bnFSHH

The United Federation Marine Corps

Recruit

Sergeant

Lieutenant

Captain

Major

Lieutenant Colonel

Colonel

Commandant

Rebel

(Set in the UFMC universe.)

Behind Enemy Lines

(A UFMC Prequel)

The Accidental War (A Ryck Lysander Short Story Published in *BOB's Bar: Tales from the Multiverse*)

The United Federation Marine Corps' Lysander Twins

Legacy Marines
Esther's Story: Recon Marine
Noah's Story: Marine Tanker
Esther's Story: Special Duty
Blood United

Coda

Women of the United Federation Marine Corps

Gladiator
Sniper
Corpsman

High Value Target (A Gracie Medicine Crow Short Story)
BOLO Mission (A Gracie Medicine Crow Short Story)
Weaponized Math (A Gracie Medicine Crow Novelette, First published in *The Expanding Universe 3:* 2017 Nebula Award Finalist)

The United Federation Marine Corps' Grub Wars

Alliance
The Price of Honor
Division of Power

The Navy of Humankind: Wasp Squadron
Fire Ant
Crystals

Ghost Marines
Integration (2018 Dragon Award Finalist)
Unification
Fusion

The Return of the Marines Trilogy
The Few
The Proud
The Marines

The Al Anbar Chronicles: First Marine Expeditionary Force--Iraq
Prisoner of Fallujah
Combat Corpsman
Sniper

Werewolf of Marines
Werewolf of Marines: Semper Lycanus
Werewolf of Marines: Patria Lycanus
Werewolf of Marines: Pax Lycanus

To the Shores of Tripoli

Wererat

Darwin's Quest: The Search for the Ultimate Survivor

Assorted Short Stories

Venus: A Paleolithic Short Story
Secession
Duty
Semper Fidelis
Checkmate (Published in the *Expanding Universe 4*)

Non-Fiction

Exercise for a Longer Life

The Effects of Environmental Activism on the Tuna
Industry

Nuclear Proliferation: Will Japan and Germany Join
the Club? (Published in *the Journal of International
Studies*)

Author Website
http://www.jonathanbrazee.com

The Amazing Conroy is back!

Conroy takes Reggie, his alien companion animal, to visit a casino hotel on Titan. Their objective: an illegal auction for the galaxy's rarest liquor.

But hijinx ensue wherever a former stage hypnotist shows up with an animal that can eat anything and farts oxygen.

An excerpt from the Nebula Award finalist:

Barry's Deal

Lawrence M. Schoen

Most security scans mistake buffalo dogs for bombs — really powerful bombs — and respond with a cacophony of alarms. Which is why I'd pulled Reggie from my carpet bag where he'd been since we disembarked and carried him under one arm. The bag took its place in the queue of the security scanner and we waited our turn in the customs line for the Higgins arcology on Triton, a hypnotist-turned CEO and his alien companion animal. We were fourth from the front, my bag just short of the scanner housing, when sirens began blaring and lights started flashing. My buffalito turned his head and gave me a look of utter innocence, but I knew Reggie wasn't responsible for the ruckus.

Which meant that someone ahead of us had attempted to smuggle a bomb into the pressurized city of the arcology.

A three-person security squad jumped into action, wrestling the couple at the front of the line to the ground. It was only after taking them down that they saw their error. They'd have been better served tackling the third person, the fellow who now had one hand wrapped around a black cylinder about the size of a roll of quarters with a shiny red button on the top and his thumb alongside the button. He reached into the scanner housing, yanking free the briefcase that had triggered the alarm. He hugged it to his chest as he shouted something in a language I didn't know.

When he pressed the red button an automated voice began speaking softly in Traveler — which I did understand — a string of descending numbers, a countdown. It had started at sixty.

Around me people screamed, pointed, ran away, or some combination of the three. I wasn't so much standing my ground as trying to contain a panicking buffalito who moments before had been napping. In front of me, my old friend LeftJohn Mocker muttered "what are the odds?" seconds before he tapped our would-be bomber on the shoulder from behind. The man whirled and LeftJohn punched him in the face. He landed a second blow to the man's solar plexus and stomped on his ankle for good measure. The detonator tumbled through the air and LeftJohn grabbed the briefcase. Bomber guy lunged to reclaim it and LeftJohn struck him with it. The impact caused the case's latch to pop and the lid sprang open. A grey-green ceramic box with a gleaming countdown display that matched the spoken one flew from it. The Mocker caught it and handed it to me.

"Here, deal with this."

"I don't want the bomb!"

"Not you. Reggie."

"Right!"

I juggled my buffalito around and presented the bomb to him. "Come on, boy, time for lunch."

Obligingly he opened wide and leaned in, closing his mouth around a corner of the box. He bit through it as if it were meringue. The counter had dropped down to the forties.

"I need you to eat a bit quicker. Fast food, Reggie."

Two bites later and a new siren joined the noise. If I were a betting man I'd have said Reggie had bitten through some shielding and now radiation was pouring through. I pressed the remains of the box into his mouth, encouraging him to eat faster. He finished it with time to spare and beamed at me as I praised him. I also kept one hand on his muzzle to keep his mouth closed until I was sure he'd swallowed everything. Whatever fissionable bits had once been a bomb were now safe and secure inside his stomach. The same alien hide that made buffalitos impenetrable to external scans also kept anything unpleasant from leaking out.

To read more of Barry's Deal, click here.